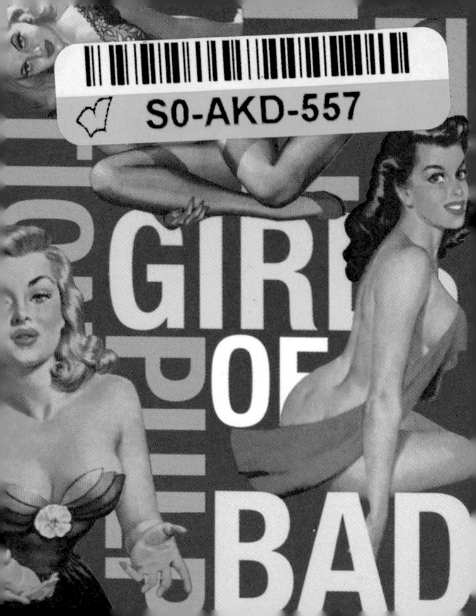
OF
BAD

BAD GIRLS OF PULP FICTION

A Running Press® Miniature Edition™

Printed in China

Library of Congress Cataloging-in-Publication Number 2001094159

ISBN 0-7624-1256-9

Postcards may be ordered from the PC Design website:
www.pulpcards.com

This book may be ordered by mail from the publisher.
Please include $1.00 for postage and handling.
But try your bookstore first!

Running Press Book Publishers
125 South Twenty-second Street
Philadelphia, Pennsylvania 19103-4399

Visit us on the web!
www.runningpress.com

BAD GIRLS OF PULP FICTION

RUNNING PRESS
PHILADELPHIA • LONDON

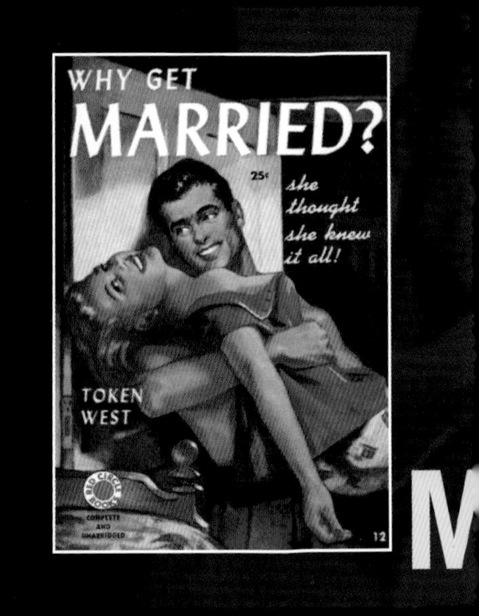
WHY GET
MARRIED?
25¢
she
thought
she knew
it all!
TOKEN
WEST
RED CIRCLE BOOKS
COMPLETE
AND
UNABRIDGED
12
M

Because if you loved someone—if you really loved someone and knew that you'd always stay together—well, wasn't that enough? Caroline knew that it was. "All right," she told him, "but only if you *promise* to wear two of them."

WHY GET ARRIED?

HOW CHEAP CAN YOU GET?

Molly and Nancy knew
their place in life—
they knew they were cheaper
than penny candy—but a small part
of them still wondered:
How cheap can you *really* get?
How low could you *really* go?
And how good would it
make you feel?

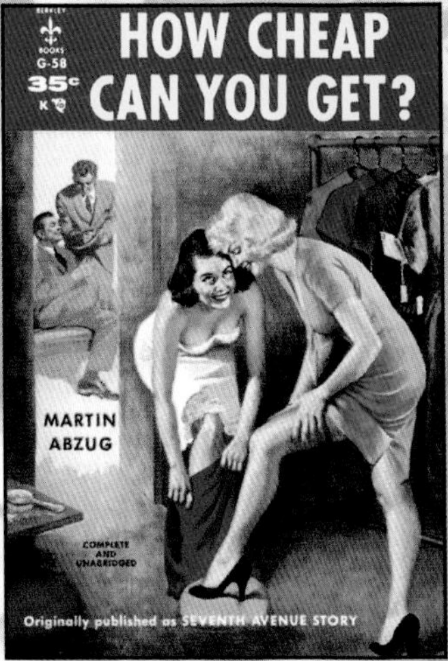
BERKLEY
BOOKS
G-58
35c
K
HOW CHEAP CAN YOU GET?
MARTIN
ABZUG
COMPLETE
AND
UNABRIDGED
Originally published as SEVENTH AVENUE STORY

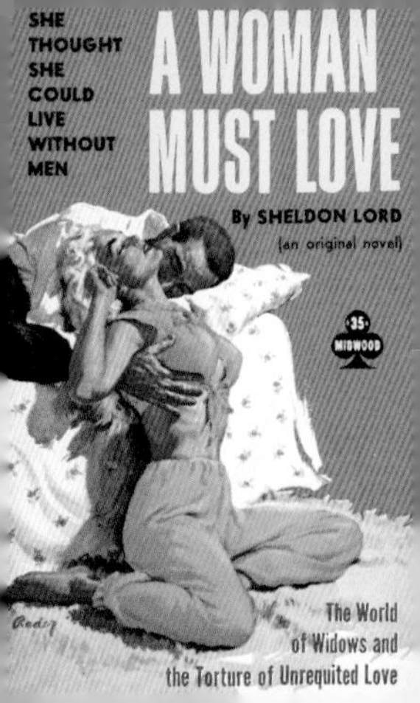
SHE THOUGHT SHE COULD LIVE WITHOUT MEN
A WOMAN MUST LOVE
By SHELDON LORD
(an original novel)
35
MIDWOOD
The World of Widows and the Torture of Unrequited Love

A WOMAN MUST LOVE

Still, there were nights when Mary Ann felt lonely. And then there were nights when unmentionable instincts surfaced inside her, rising like a red-hot molten lava. How long would she go on ignoring them? And who would be the first man to get burned?

K

50¢

MIDWOOD

F230

UNCENSORED EDITION

TAKE ME

It took her a long time to say it, but when she did – that is where this story begins.

By JOHN B. THOMPSON

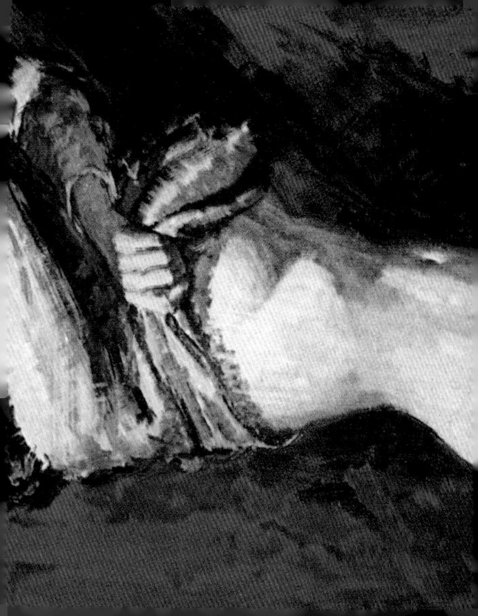

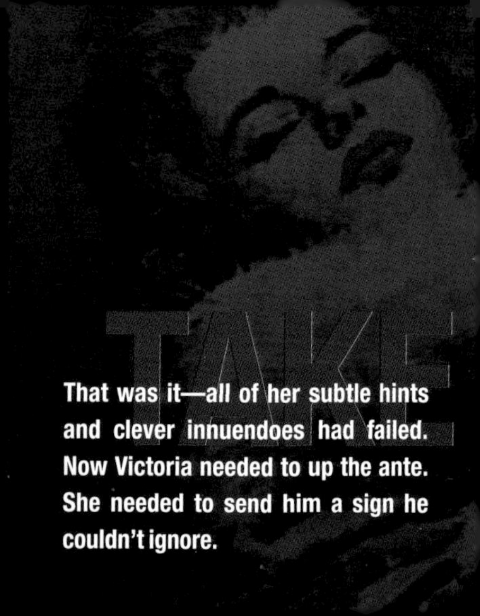

TAKE

That was it—*all* of her subtle hints and clever innuendoes had failed. Now Victoria needed to up the ante. She needed to send him a sign he couldn't ignore.

ME

When this woman wanted love, she knew what to do—
Dial "M" for Man
B465F
50¢
K
ORRIE HITT
Hob Sampson was a local businessman who walked in on trouble every time a lonely wife like Doris Condon phoned for help. The beautiful Mrs. Condon's husband left her cold—and she wanted a man around the house day and night!
BEHIND THE "RESPECTABLE" FRONT DOOR IN SUBURBIA

Who should it be this time?

The electrician?

The milkman? Or maybe the lawn boy?

Each had his own strengths

and weaknesses, and

choosing one was difficult.

But then a brilliant idea occurred to her:

"Why," Doris asked herself,

"do I need to choose just one?"

CONFESSIONS OF A PSYCHIATRIST

Anne knew something was wrong: What kind of psychiatrist asked his patients to undress on their first visit? As the cold cup of the stethoscope pressed against her thigh, she shivered and tried to remain calm. . . .

EVERY BOUDOIR WAS HIS OFFICE:
EVERY PATIENT HIS PLAYTHING—
CONFESSIONS of a
PSYCHIATRIST
35¢
B184
by Henry Lewis Nixon
A BEACON FIRST AWARD ORIGINAL NOVEL!

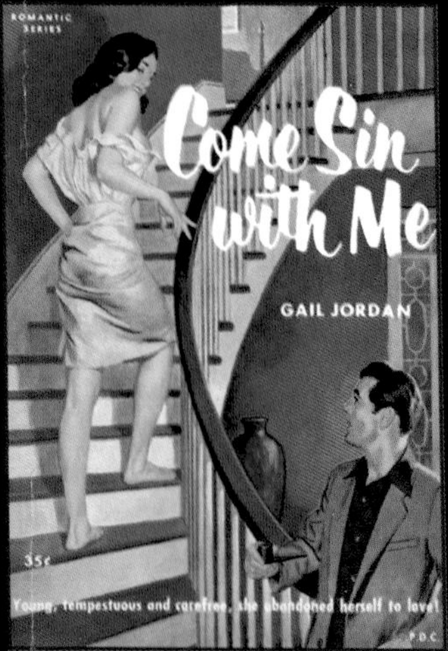
ROMANTIC SERIES
Come Sin with Me
GAIL JORDAN
35¢
Young, tempestuous and carefree, she abandoned herself to love!
P.D.C.

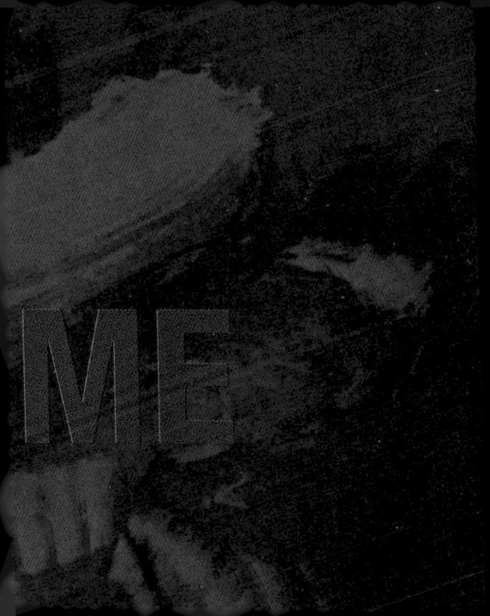
ME

When this woman wanted love, she knew what to do—
Dial "M" for Man
B465F
50¢
ORRIE HITT
Hob Sampson was a local business-man who walked in on trouble every time a lonely wife like Doris Condon phoned
The beautiful Mrs. Condon's husband left her cold—and she wanted a man around the house day and night!
BEHIND THE "RESPECTABLE" FRONT DOOR IN SUBURBIA

It occurred to Jennifer
that she was
only nineteen but had already
broken most of
the ten commandments.
She was a petty thief. She lied
to her parents.
And she honored false gods.
So why stop there?
She extended her hand to Phillip
and whispered sultrily,
"Come, my sweet."

Melissa knew she must not go upstairs with him. She could hear her mother's voice, warning her about temptation. But then she slammed her hands against her ears... blocking out the voice, until there was nothing left but silence. Silence, and the low steady growl of his loins...

SATA
WAS A MAN

N

A Surging Novel Of Passion And Ruin 25c
SATAN WAS A MAN
Edward Hale Bierstadt
Complete and Unabridged

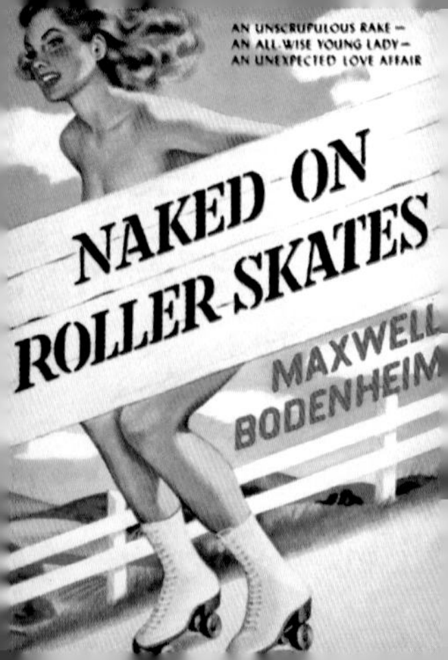
AN UNSCRUPULOUS RAKE —
AN ALL-WISE YOUNG LADY —
AN UNEXPECTED LOVE AFFAIR
NAKED ON
ROLLER SKATES
MAXWELL
BODENHEIM

Swooooosh!
Danni raced down the hill,
zooming past confused bystanders,
bending her knees and leaning
into the wind and feeling the warmth
of the sun on her body.

"This!" she cried out.
"This is what it means to be alive!"

MEN ARE SUCH FOOLS

Didn't he recognize
the love of a good woman?
How could he be so blind? How could
he be so stupid? And why
had *she* given so much of herself
to such a blind, stupid,
unworthy man?

138
men
are such fools
A DELL BOOK
DELL
A DELL BOOK
by FAITH
BALDWIN
COMPLETE WITH
MAP ON
BACK COVER
NO.
138
A DELL ROMANCE

It Was Wrong To Be Bad, BUT—
SHE COULDN'T
BE
GOOD!
VENUS BOOKS
A BRAND NEW NOVEL! NEVER PUBLISHED BEFORE!

There was a time when Susan *was* good. A time of church on Sundays and holding hands and ice cream sodas at McGinty's drugstore. But nowadays, she only visited a drugstore to buy implements of sin, and Old Man McGinty blushed at the very sight of her.

So there it was, the most important night of Julie's life, the night she'd always saved herself for. And yet it had ended so quickly. It was all so disappointing. Her new husband lay beside her, deep in slumber, almost comatose. Almost like a dead man, Julie thought.

I MARRIED A DEAD M

THE STRANGE STORY OF A GIRL WHO IS
BOTH BRIDE AND WIDOW AND YET NOT EITHER
I MARRIED A DEAD MAN
COMPLETE AND UNABRIDGED
William Irish

AN

TAKE IT
AND
LIKE
IT
AN ARCHER BOOK
by
SPIKE
MORELLI
with the gloves off
2/6D
PRICE IN U.S.A.
35¢
AND CANADA

BAD
GIRLS
OF
PULP
FICTION

TAKE IT AND LIKE IT

Amie had always
been a bad girl, dominating
but delighting the men she seduced.
But what happens
when the roles are reversed?
Can she take what
she gives? Jimmy is about to find out,
whether Amie likes it or not.

433

MONARCH BOOKS

40¢

She Was Wild And Willing—
But She Played For Keeps

KISS ME QUICK

Karl Kramer

Lindsay eyed the man across the room. She had given herself to him. Together they had lived each other's fantasies. It broke her heart to see him with another woman, but more than that, it inflamed her jealous passions. She was not about to take this lying down, like she had so many other men's affairs before. This time, she would fight back.

ME

SHE TRADED HER BODY FOR DRUGS— AND KICKS!
Marijuana Girl
N. R. DeMexico
B328
35¢
NEVER WAS THERE SO OUTSPOKEN A NOVEL AS THIS . . . TELLING THE PLAIN, UNCENSORED TRUTH ABOUT TEEN-AGE ADDICTS — AND THEIR DESPERATE SEARCH FOR THRILLS!

MARIJUANA GIRL

Once a well-behaved schoolgirl, Kate started doing drugs at parties—just once in awhile. What started as an innocent experiment became a life of fast times with a dangerous crowd. Now, she's out of control and will do anything to feed her addictions . . . ANYTHING!

Catherine had no problem being friendly towards the women on her street—and then sleeping with their husbands. She just wasn't interested in men who were unattached. So she batted her eyelashes and showed a little skin, and they were hers. All of them. But, as Catherine soon finds out, back-stabbing and betrayal don't come cheap.

A LADIES MAN — A NAUGHTY WIFE — A WICKED MISTRESS
NL
18
BEDROOM EYES
MAURICE DEKOBRA

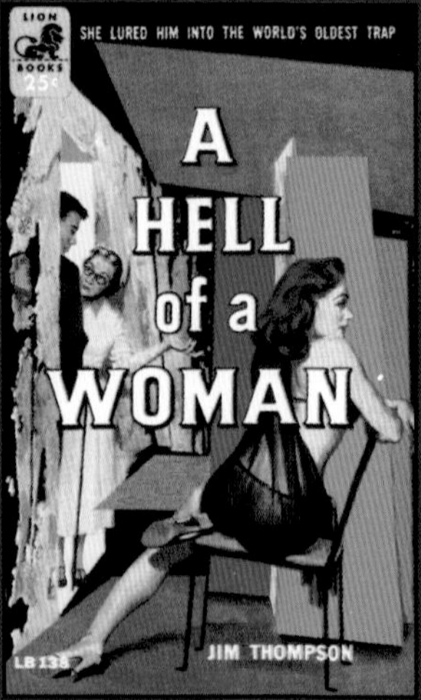
LION BOOKS
25¢
SHE LURED HIM INTO THE WORLD'S OLDEST TRAP
A HELL of a WOMAN
LB 138
JIM THOMPSON

Greg never suspected anything.
His friends all joked that
he was quite the playboy; he fell in and
out of love quickly and regularly.
But tonight would be different.
Tonight, Greg will meet a woman
who will lead him down a twisted trail
of seduction, lies, and lust.
If he's not careful, Greg may
find himself trapped with
A Hell of a Woman.

Temptress Tip:

When picking out the perfect outfit, note that a little cleavage goes a long way. Wearing a blouse or dress with a plunging neckline isn't trashy, it shows you're using your head! Show just enough of your assets to keep heads turning, but never too much to break a man's neck. Remember, you've got to give a little to get a little.

SHE WAS A PAWN IN AN EVIL GAME.
LUST IS A WOMAN
By Charles Williford
THE STORY OF MARIA WHO WANTED
—DESPERATELY—TO BECOME A MOVIE STAR!

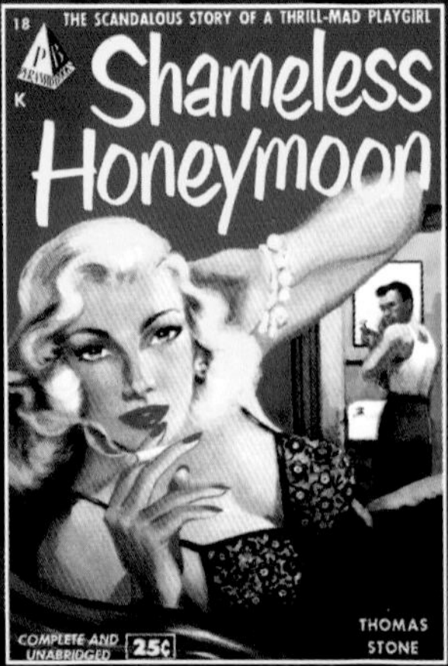
18
K
THE SCANDALOUS STORY OF A THRILL-MAD PLAYGIRL
Shameless Honeymoon
COMPLETE AND UNABRIDGED
25¢
THOMAS STONE

Wild and passionate,
Adrianne was a playgirl who lived
for men, cheap booze, and
nights on the town.
Everyone thought that once she
settled down, Adrianne would
finally become a proper young lady.
But as they soon find out,
not even marriage can stop
a thrill-crazy gal from getting
what she wants.

CARNIVAL OF LOVE

New Orleans. Amidst the festival of lust and intoxication that is Mardi Gras, Alicia meets the man of her dreams. They spend the week together, making each other's dreams come true. But Mardi Gras is a celebration of temptation, and Alicia is about to meet that temptation face-to-face, and see if she can stare it down.

IT HAPPENED IN NEW ORLEANS...
CARNIVAL of LOVE
Anthony Scott
25¢
RED CIRCLE BOOKS
COMPLETE and UNABRIDGED
13

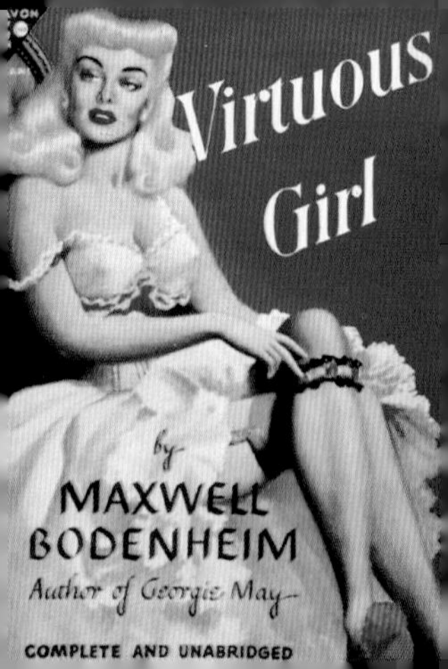
Virtuous
Girl
by
MAXWELL
BODENHEIM
Author of Georgie May
COMPLETE AND UNABRIDGED

Jessica doesn't smoke
or drink, and she's
saving herself for marriage . . .
or at least that's what she claims
until Reilly waltzes
into her life. With his sweet talk
and firm young body, Reilly
sweeps Jessica off her feet.
Once she forgets her
righteous past, Jessica opens
her eyes to a shameful
world of pleasure.

They were expensive hookers
who lived in luxurious apartments,
smoked expensive cigarettes,
and drank only the best liquor.
Dominique and Tanya flaunted their
money and made all the other hussies
rage with jealousy. But no one,
harlot or john, could guess
that these girls weren't just
objects of desire—but weapons
of death as well . . .

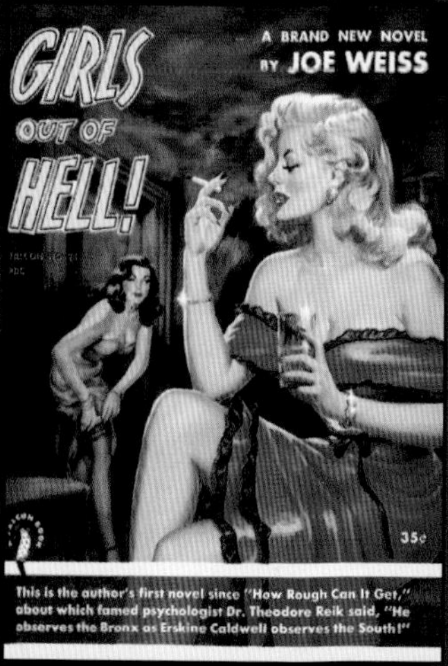
GIRLS OUT OF HELL!
A BRAND NEW NOVEL
BY JOE WEISS
35¢
This is the author's first novel since "How Rough Can It Get," about which famed psychologist Dr. Theodore Reik said, "He observes the Bronx as Erskine Caldwell observes the South!"

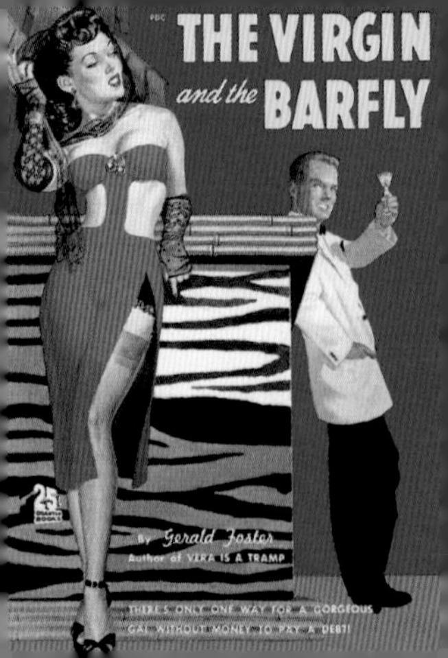
PDC
THE VIRGIN
and the BARFLY
By Gerald Foster
Author of VERA IS A TRAMP
THERE'S ONLY ONE WAY FOR A GORGEOUS
GAL WITHOUT MONEY TO PAY A DEBT!

THE VIRGIN AND THE BARFLY

Diana walked into the bar, her heart beating faster and faster. She scanned the faces of the men whose eyes ran all over her voluptuous body, searching for him. Eventually her hungry gaze sought him out, there on the stool where she usually found him. Diana couldn't help herself around Greg—even though he didn't do much but drink, she simply had to have him. And he had to be the first.

Casey was nothing if not a party girl; she liked her music loud, her liquor cold, and her men ready. She kept things casual and made sure she never got too personal. She loved bongos almost as much as she loved men—but then she met Brian, and all that changed. He was tall, dark, handsome . . . and *trouble.*

LIKE CRAZY, MAN!

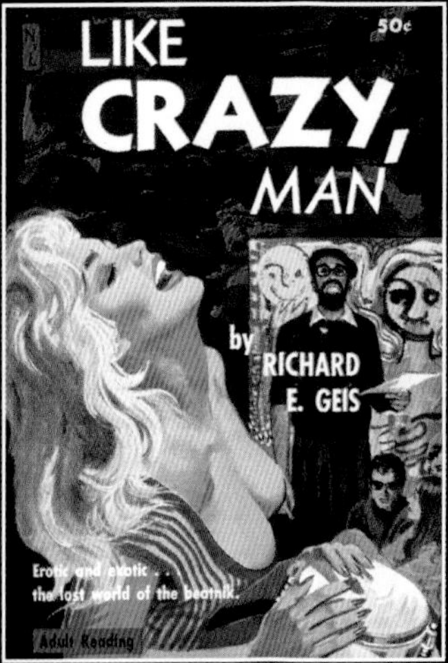
50¢
LIKE
CRAZY,
MAN
by
RICHARD
E. GEIS
Erotic and exotic . . .
the lost world of the beatnik.
Adult Reading

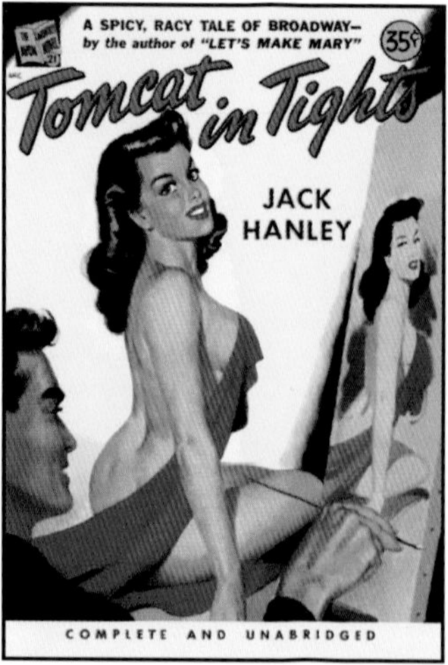
A SPICY, RACY TALE OF BROADWAY—
by the author of "LET'S MAKE MARY"
35¢
Tomcat in Tights
JACK
HANLEY
COMPLETE AND UNABRIDGED

TOMCAT IN TIGHTS

Temptress Tip:

When walking in four-inch heels, make sure to swing your hips slowly. Do it too fast and you look like an electric toy, but do it slow and you're beckoning to him with your sway. Believe me, he'll answer the call!

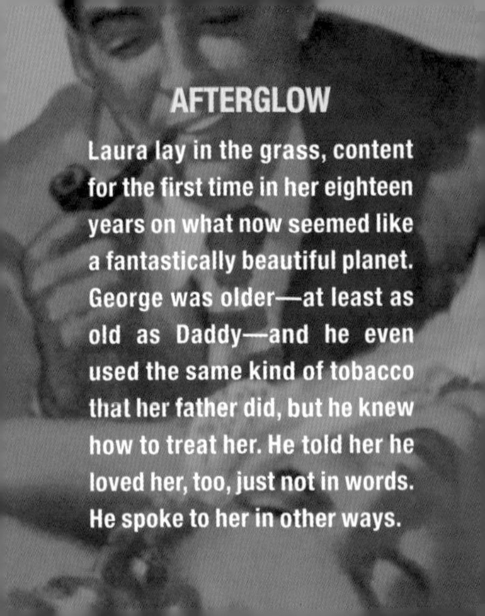

AFTERGLOW

Laura lay in the grass, content for the first time in her eighteen years on what now seemed like a fantastically beautiful planet. George was older—at least as old as Daddy—and he even used the same kind of tobacco that her father did, but he knew how to treat her. He told her he loved her, too, just not in words. He spoke to her in other ways.

A DELL BOOK
DELL
336
Afterglow
Ruby M. Ayres

She just didn't know how to say no to a man.
That's why she was
ANYBODY'S GIRL
By
MARCH HASTINGS
(an original story)
35¢
MIDWOOD
A brutally frank story of a girl who was
a helpless victim of her own passions

It didn't take much;
a smile, a glance, a brief gesture—
even just an unintentional touch.
Frannie wasn't choosy and
she didn't say no. She said yes, yes,
YES, and she said it a lot. All a man had
to do was come near her and
her resolve to change her easy ways
fell apart the way her dress did when
he pulled her to him . . .

ONE NIGHT WITH NANCY

She woke up around noon,
and wasn't surprised to find herself
blissfully alone. He must
have left sometime during the night,
just slipped out of her silky sheets
and out the door. That was fine
with Nancy; she didn't want
more than one night with any man.
One night was enough—to turn
them on and turn them inside out,
and then be done with them.

20
A BEAUTIFUL GIRL—AN AMOROUS MALE—A GREAT WEEKEND
ONE NIGHT with NANCY
Wilson Collison
COMPLETE AND UNABRIDGED

Passion Has Red Lips
PDC
No. 108
35¢

Temptress Tip:

When applying lipstick on the go, take time to tease. Grab a spoon or small mirror, and slowly unscrew the stick while licking your lips slightly. Languorously smear the war paint over your top and bottom lips before pressing them together for the perfect pout.

PASSION HAS

D LIPS

HELP WANTED—MALE

Kay knew
she needed a man,
but she couldn't decide
what sort. She loved them ALL.
This time, she thought,
I'll get specific.
"Wanted: MALE. I don't care
what you're into or what you do,
but I need a special kind
of love, and you better be able
to give it to me,"
she wrote on the ad form.
She was on her way!

NC 41
WANTED—SOMEONE TO GIVE ME
MY SPECIAL KIND OF LOVE
HELP WANTED-MALE
COMPLETE AND UNABRIDGED
THOMAS STONE

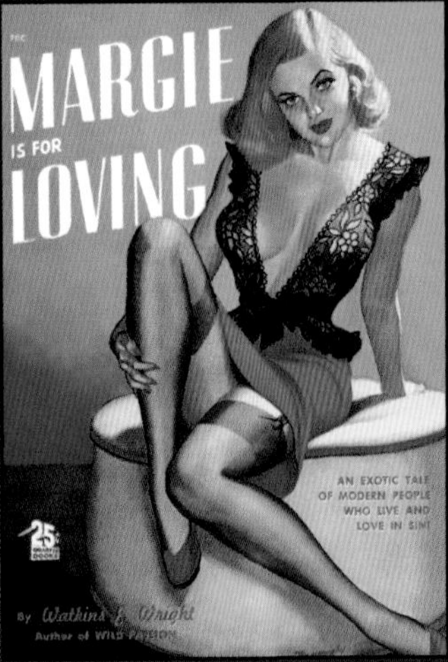
MARGIE
IS FOR
LOVING
AN EXOTIC TALE OF MODERN PEOPLE WHO LIVE AND LOVE IN SIN!
25¢
By Watkins E. Wright
Author of WILD PASSION

MARGIE IS FOR LOVING

It was all she could do to get through a day without loving. Margie needed constant caressing, kissing, and cuddling. Without it she couldn't bear to be alive. So she took it where she could get it. Friends and coworkers called her easy, desperate, but they didn't understand. They didn't know what she knew, that her purpose was *for* love, that her job was *to* love.

Amanda knew she had talent—that wasn't the problem. Her problem was that no one would take her work seriously. They thought she was just a pretty face, a tight body. She had to make them realize that her art *meant* something, that it really was worth considering, no matter what she looked like. She eventually came to realize that the only way to make them see was to play their game, so she unbuttoned her blouse, put her paintbrush between her teeth, and marched into his office.

Bohemian love, erotic artists, underworld trysts and passionate ambition all play a part in the notorious adventures of a . . .
GREENWICH VILLAGE
Girl

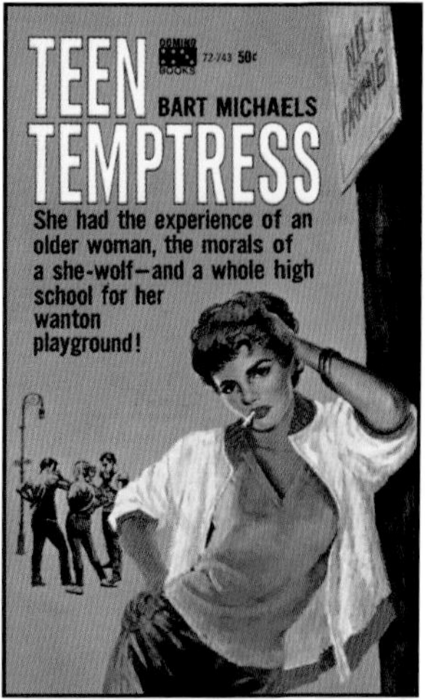
TEEN TEMPTRESS
DOMINO BOOKS
72-743 50¢
BART MICHAELS
She had the experience of an older woman, the morals of a she-wolf—and a whole high school for her wanton playground!

TEEN
TEMPTRESS

Dina had been around the block—
a few times. She knew people
thought she was bad, and she *was* bad.
She didn't mind what people
said behind her back, or
even to her face, because she got
what she wanted. Every time.
And this time, what she wanted
was Mr. Holden, her English teacher.
She would get him, too.

Amy had always been jealous of her sister, and she didn't try to hide it. Instead of making her own way, she grabbed what she could, even when it belonged to Nicole, her older sister. Especially when it belonged to her. Take Derek, for example. Or Harry. Or Len. She'd gotten them all, hadn't she? And it was as easy as taking candy from a baby. Richard would be just as easy, she was sure of it.

345
MONARCH BOOKS 35¢
She wanted a man just like her sister had — so she took him
LIKE WILD
Eric Allen
First Publication Anywhere

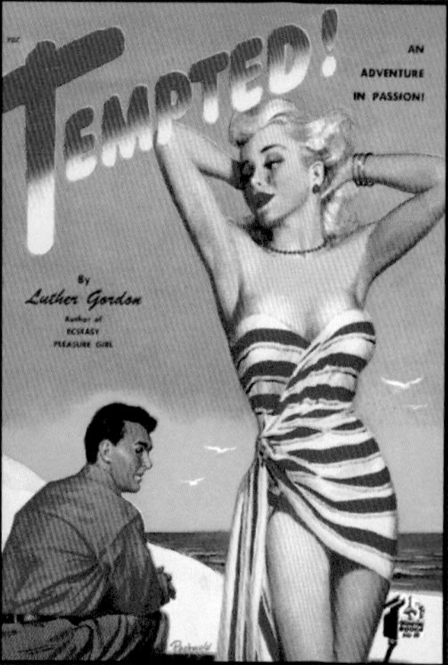
TEMPTED!
AN ADVENTURE IN PASSION!
By
Luther Gordon
Author of
ECSTASY
PLEASURE GIRL

TEMPTED!

Temptress Tips

At the beach, a lady always makes sure she's properly covered, but a temptress can show some skin! The best way to be the first girl noticed is to wear your hair tied back and a sarong with your suit, then shake your hair out from its binding ever so slowly, swinging it to and fro. Then unwrap yourself from the sarong in that same languid way, like you have all the time in the world.

STRANGE SISTERS

"You know just what
a woman wants," said Grace.
"You make me feel
beautiful, sexy, needed. . .
Lance could never do that."
She looked her lover
in the eyes, deep pools of blue.

"All we need is someone
who understands,"
Sandra replied. "Sometimes,
it takes a woman."

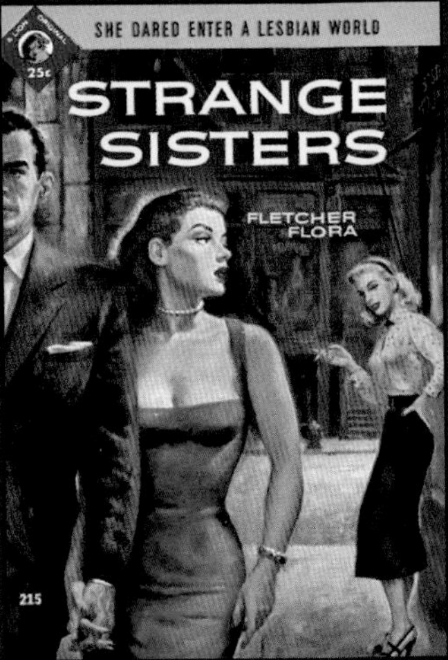
SHE DARED ENTER A LESBIAN WORLD
25¢
STRANGE SISTERS
FLETCHER FLORA
215

Plaything of Passion
PRICE IN U.S.A. 35¢ AND CANADA
Mad, unholy desire, strange diabolical hate and an all-consuming love reveals itself in this novel
JEANETTE REVÉRE
PLAYTHING

OF PASSION

PRICE IN U.S.A. AND CANADA 35¢

"Touch me," Alice thought. "I just want you to touch me, is that too much to ask?" She longed for him as he stood in the doorway watching her. Then her slipper fell from her foot onto the floor. Her dress followed as it slid off her shoulders and crumpled about her ankles. Finally he moved toward her as she spread herself on the bed . . .

"You shouldn't hang around with that crowd," Marcy told her older sister. "They are high school drop-outs, drug addicts, and womanizers," she advised.

"Well, maybe that's the way I like them," Debbie retorted. "Maybe little girls like you just can't understand." She flashed a wicked smile and tramped out the door.

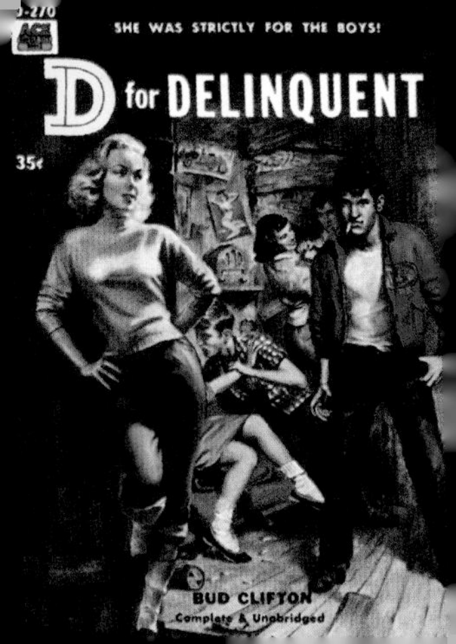
SHE WAS STRICTLY FOR THE BOYS!
D for DELINQUENT
35¢
BUD CLIFTON
Complete & Unabridged

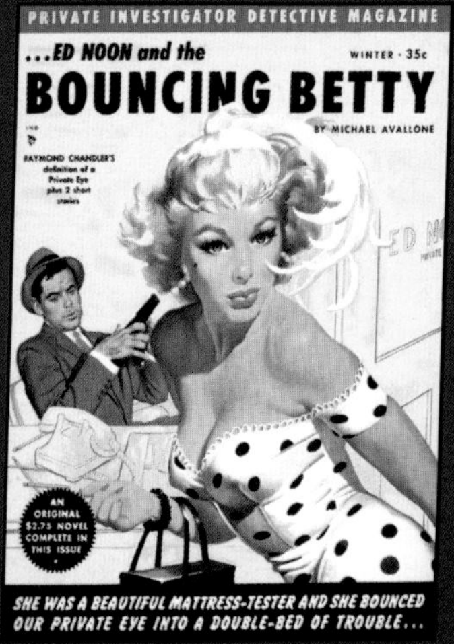
PRIVATE INVESTIGATOR DETECTIVE MAGAZINE
...ED NOON and the
WINTER · 35c
BOUNCING BETTY
BY MICHAEL AVALLONE
RAYMOND CHANDLER'S definition of a Private Eye plus 2 short stories
AN ORIGINAL $2.75 NOVEL COMPLETE IN THIS ISSUE
SHE WAS A BEAUTIFUL MATTRESS-TESTER AND SHE BOUNCED OUR PRIVATE EYE INTO A DOUBLE-BED OF TROUBLE...

BOUNCING BETTY

"I'm a working girl," she explained. "I test mattresses."

"You don't say. Is that a science?" teased Detective Claude.

"Sure," Betty said. "I look for comfort, durability, strength—of course to collect acceptable data, I must be completely naked. Care for a demonstration?"

How could a loving housewife and mother of three just run off one day? Patty left her family, friends, and neighbors shocked and questioning when she ran off to the big city—with a man she met at the grocery store! He bought her expensive clothes and drove her around town in his flashy car. And he made sure he got something in return. But when Patty wanted out, she learned that being a slave of passion is not temporary work.

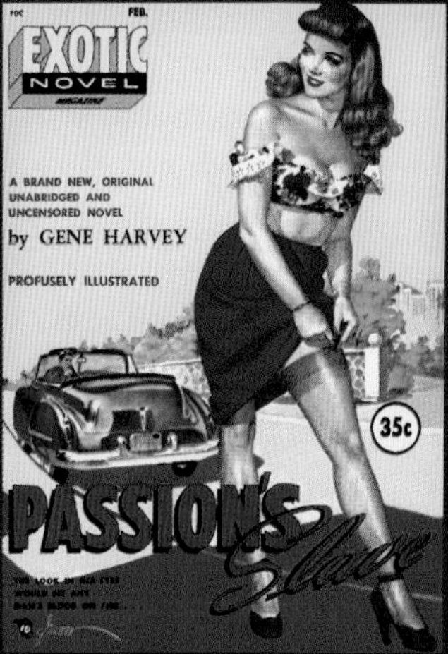
FEB.
EXOTIC
NOVEL
A BRAND NEW, ORIGINAL
UNABRIDGED AND
UNCENSORED NOVEL
by GENE HARVEY
PROFUSELY ILLUSTRATED
35c
PASSION'S
Slave

POPULAR LIBRARY
What Husbands Don't Know Won't Hurt Them
A Woman of Forty
DESMOND HALL
Complete and Unabridged

They embraced
in the darkened living room,
holding each other close . . . then closer.
"I'm old enough to be your mother,"
Judith whispered in his ear.

"Relax, Mrs. Bower," Tony said
as he took off his shirt. "Your husband
will never find out. Besides,
you know you want it," he urged,
gently stroking her thigh.

"Yes," she admitted,
leaning towards him. "Yes, I do."

Temptress Tip:

Every woman knows what she wants, but a temptress knows exactly how to get it. Be bold. Be daring. Be a little naughty. When going after your guy, modesty is never an option. Get his attention with a quick glance, but keep him guessing with a long, deep stare. When he goes for the bait, reel him in like the catch that he is.

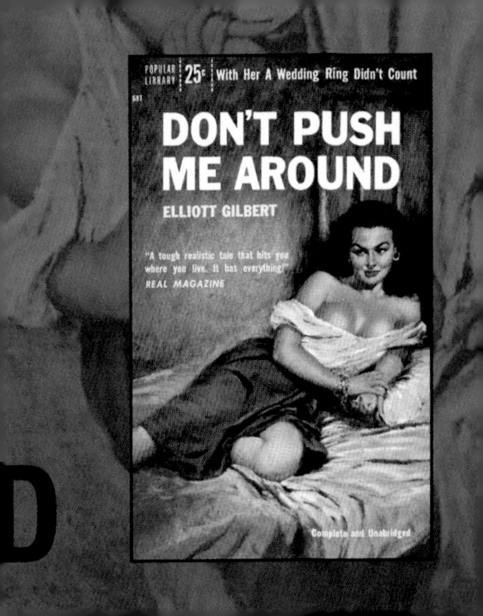
POPULAR LIBRARY
25¢
With Her A Wedding Ring Didn't Count
DON'T PUSH ME AROUND
ELLIOTT GILBERT
"A tough realistic tale that hits you where you live. It has everything!"
REAL MAGAZINE
Complete and Unabridged
D

A TERROR IN THE RING...
A TIGRESS IN THE BOUDOIR!
LOVES OF A
GIRL
WRESTLER
BEN WEST
35¢
K
B357
MAULED . . . MANHANDLED . . . EXHIBITED BEFORE LUSTING EYES . . . THIS LOVELY CREATURE FOUGHT DEPRAVITY AND DISGRACE AT THE HANDS OF BONE-CRUSHING MEN AND PASSIONATE AMAZONS

L
GIR

Ha! She had him in a half-nelson, and Kelly wasn't about to let go! She had him just where she'd always wanted him, and she couldn't give up. Not now, not when she was so close to making him admit that he loved her too! She looked down at his shiny black hair, saw the look of pain on his face, but—could it be?—also a look of tenderness. "SAY IT!" she screeched.

SEX-A-GO-GO

Janeen walked into the club and felt her heart rise up into her throat. There he was! Dick Dynamite—the lead singer! He was beautiful without a shirt on, just as she had known he would be. She began to salivate as he strummed the guitar in his lap, and then her fingers went to the buttons of her blouse, and began unbuttoning. It was as if they worked with a lust all their own!

W-22
95c
EB
SEX-A-GOGO
By RUSS TRAINER
EXOTIK BOOK COLLECTORS EDITION

GLORIA — MADELINE — SANDY!
EACH WAS EASY PICKIN'S
PUSHOVER
by Orrie Hitt
35¢
B 380
THE TORRID TALE
OF A TOWN MORE
WICKED THAN
PEYTON PLACE!
BEACON

Rex pushed her down, kissed her roughly. Gloria knew better than to like it, but she liked it anyway. She kissed him back, which only angered him more, and he grabbed her hair.

"I hate you!" Gloria hissed, a glint in her eye, a small smile playing on her inflamed lips.

"I know you do," Rex sneered. "But you love this."

"Mmmm . . . You're so right."

"I've been a showgirl
since I was sixteen," she said. "It's easy
money, and I'm the best."

"You're beautiful," the stranger replied.
"I can certainly see why
they call you 'Desire.' Would you like
to go out for a drink?"

She looked him up and down.
"Well, I'm not supposed
to see customers outside the club,
but maybe just tonight . . ."

50¢
I Am Desire
Varieties of love—from the woman's point of view.
The daring story of three intimate affairs.
ANONYMOUS
Special Introduction by ROBERT BRENT

SHE WAS
AVAILABLE
FOR THE
ASKING
By ADAM
ROBERTS
(AN ORIGINAL
NOVEL)
GLAD TO
BE BAD
35
MIDWOOD
Gorgeous Gwen Morgan Was Always
Willing To Give A Little To Get A Lot

TO

In today's world, nothing is ever free. Gwen knew you had to give a little to get what you wanted, and she would do anything to get what she wanted. She'd even give *a lot* if she had to. Sometimes that meant that she found herself in some very unladylike situations. But who says a "lady" can't enjoy herself once in a while?

GLAD
BE BAD

Temptress Tip:

When it's hot outside, a temptress uses the weather to her advantage! And not just by wearing a little dress, either! Get an ice-cream cone, and you might just heat him up while you cool yourself off! Lick the cone slowly and seductively, all around it—really enjoy it. He won't be able to resist, and you'll watch the sparks fly!

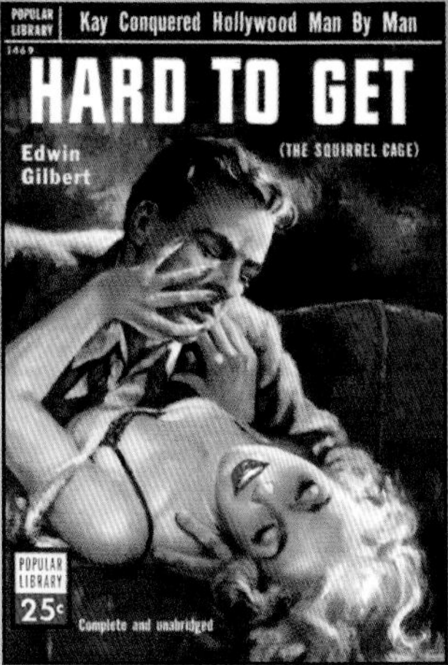
POPULAR LIBRARY
Kay Conquered Hollywood Man By Man
1469
HARD TO GET
Edwin Gilbert
(THE SQUIRREL CAGE)
POPULAR LIBRARY
25¢
Complete and unabridged

A SHAMEFUL PATH LED
HER THERE—SCARLET
SECRETS KEPT HER THERE
35¢
(HOUSE OF FURY)
REFORM
SCHOOL
GIRL
FELICE SWADOS
Diversey
Romance
Novel
1
COMPLETE AND UNABRIDGED

"That's it Ruby! I've had it up to here with your disgusting behavior. I'm recommending that you be transferred to another school, where you can become more disciplined," roared the professor.

"But Mr. Vesterman," the little tramp pouted, "then you would lose your job."

"Why is that?" he scowled.

"Because if you transfer me, I'll tell everyone about our late-night 'tutoring' sessions." She knew she had him there.

Fast cars and fast girls go hand in hand. Especially when the prize at the finish line is not a trophy or cash, but a young girl's body just aching with desire. The stakes are high, the competition is fierce, and with only one girl . . . there can only be one winner.

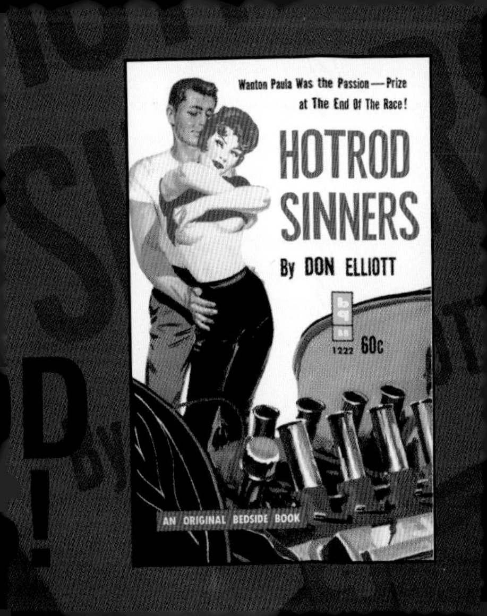
Wanton Paula Was the Passion — Prize
at The End Of The Race!
HOTROD
SINNERS
By DON ELLIOTT
bq
BB
1222 60c
AN ORIGINAL BEDSIDE BOOK

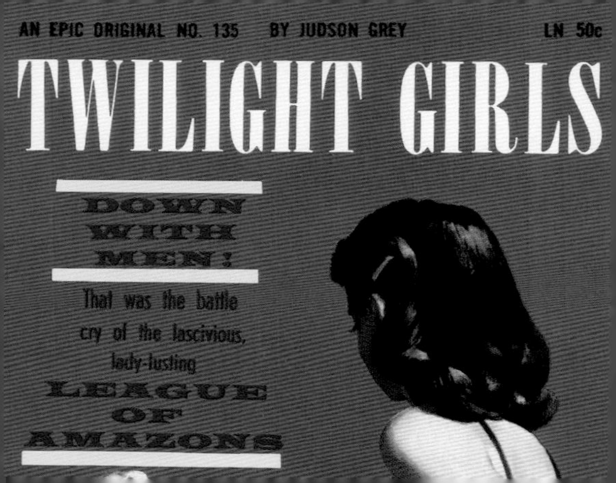
AN EPIC ORIGINAL NO. 135
BY JUDSON GREY
LN 50c
TWILIGHT GIRLS
DOWN WITH MEN!
That was the battle cry of the lascivious, lady-lusting
LEAGUE OF AMAZONS

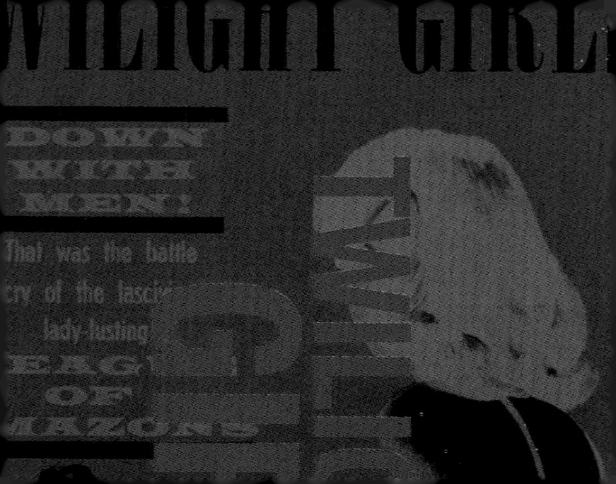
WILIGHT GIRL
DOWN
WITH
MEN!
That was the battle
cry of the lasci
lady-lusting
EAG
OF
AZONS

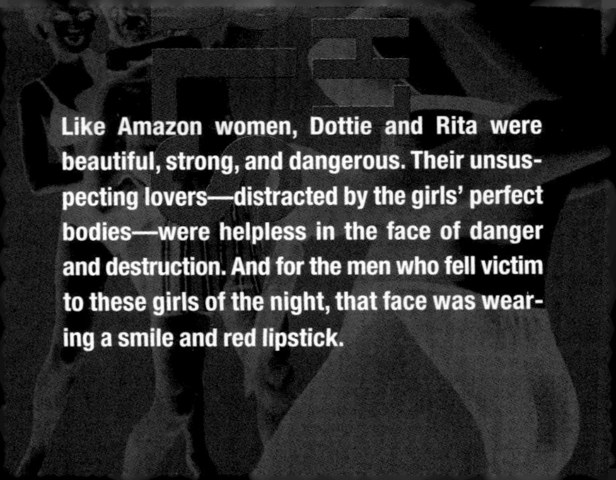

Like Amazon women, Dottie and Rita were beautiful, strong, and dangerous. Their unsuspecting lovers—distracted by the girls' perfect bodies—were helpless in the face of danger and destruction. And for the men who fell victim to these girls of the night, that face was wearing a smile and red lipstick.

QUICKIE!

"My husband will be home from work in less than an hour, do you think we should?" Samantha whispered into the phone.

"Yes, absolutely. I'm on my way," Carl replied.

"Oh well," thought Sam. "Let him find us together. I need satisfaction, and a husband of fifteen years sure isn't doing the job!"

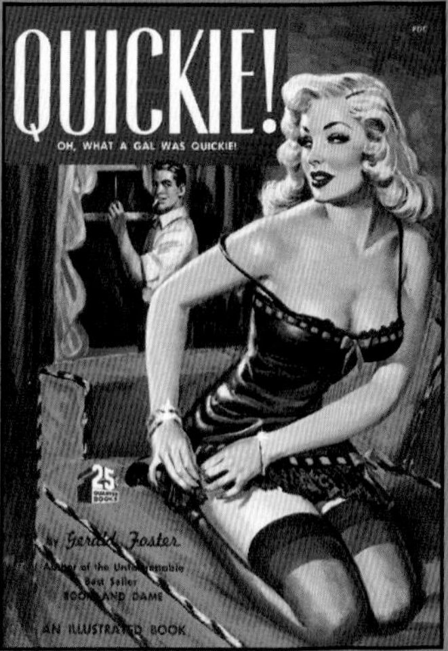
QUICKIE!
OH, WHAT A GAL WAS QUICKIE!
25
QUARTER BOOKS
Foster
Best Seller
AND DAME
AN ILLUSTRATED BOOK

FAST LOOSE, AND LOVELY

An affair with the handyman?
That would be to easy, thought Terri.
I want a challenge.
So she slept her way to the top of
her small town in New York.
Next in line, the mayor. For many, the
dream would be hopeless,
but for a girl like Terri, her man
and her challenge are always
within her grasp.

FAST, LOOSE
AND
LOVELY
A BRAND NEW NOVEL
By Norman Bligh
Author of
E FIRST,
WAYS!

DELL
35¢
The "Lady" had some very unladylike ideas—especially about Danny Fontaine's role as her bodyguard
WHEN SHE WAS BAD
by William Ard

WHEN SHE

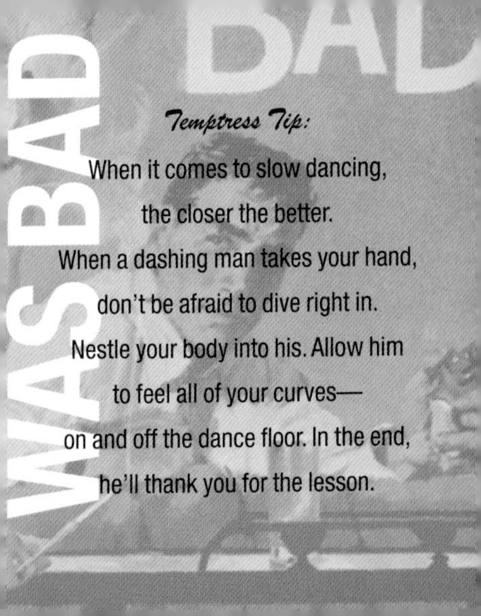

Temptress Tip:

When it comes to slow dancing, the closer the better. When a dashing man takes your hand, don't be afraid to dive right in. Nestle your body into his. Allow him to feel all of your curves—on and off the dance floor. In the end, he'll thank you for the lesson.

"Sure, I'll be your girl," Cleo replied. "But I'm not cheap."

"What could you possibly want?" Hank questioned. "You're married to the wealthiest man in New York."

MAKE M
AN OFFE

Cleo looked him in the eye and said, "A girl like me wants a lot of things. But what I want from you is a favor. I want revenge."

BERKLEY
BOOKS
G-199
35¢
MAKE ME
AN OFFER
CHARLES
GORHAM
COMPLETE
AND
UNABRIDGED
Originally published as
THE GILDED HEARSE

SHE HAD THE FACE OF AN ANGEL, THE BODY OF A DEVIL -- AND THE PASSIONS OF A LESBIAN!
THE LEATHER GIRLS

When Rhonda began experimenting with Daisy, things started off slow. Neither had been in a relationship like this before, but both knew it was what they wanted. Then Daisy started becoming more comfortable . . . too comfortable for Rhonda. She wanted whips, pain, and authority. Now, will Rhonda learn the hard way that her little angel is really a devil?

EATHER GIRLS

LSD LUSTERS

As Camille took a final hit, her eyes glazed over and she looked lustfully at Harvey.

"How do you feel?" he asked.

"I have something silly to tell you," replied the young vixen. "I want you."

"That's not silly, Camille. Let's see what we can do about that," Harvey smirked, as he led her upstairs.

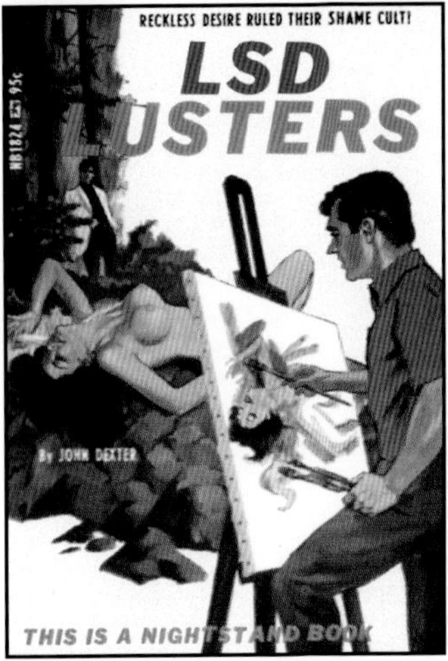
RECKLESS DESIRE RULED THEIR SHAME CULT!
LSD
LUSTERS
NB1824 95c
By JOHN DEXTER
THIS IS A NIGHTSTAND BOOK

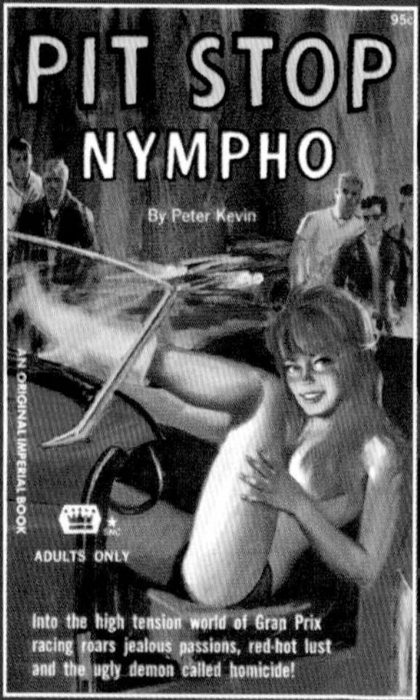
95¢
PIT STOP
NYMPHO
By Peter Kevin
AN ORIGINAL IMPERIAL BOOK
ADULTS ONLY
Into the high tension world of Gran Prix
racing roars jealous passions, red-hot lust
and the ugly demon called homicide!

PIT STOP

NYMPHO

The Grand Prix has as many secrets as it does fans. Sometimes, only a homicide can bring those secrets out into the open. When driver Chuck Neill is found brutally murdered, his wife Gina wants answers. What she finds is a hidden world full of lies, violence, money, and lust that will stop at nothing to stay hidden.

HIPPIE HARLO

She took the phrase
“Make love, not war” to heart.
This hippie chick made a lot of love
and made it with men
she barely knew. Her friends tried
their best to lead her
in the right direction. But at
Woodstock—with so many
“far out” guys around—how can
this harlot resist?

NT 829
95¢
Hippie Harlot
by Tom O'Brien
A COUGAR PUBLICATION
Adults Only
The Hippie Art Colony produced all kinds of art, but some of the by-products couldn't be shown in any Art Gallery.

This book has been bound
using handcraft methods and Smyth-
sewn to ensure durability.

The dust jacket and interior were
designed by Frances J. Soo Ping Chow.

The text was written by
Thomas J. Campbell, Nancy Armstrong,
and Jason Rekulak.

The text was edited by
Nancy Armstrong.

The text was set in Brush Script and
Helvetica Neue Condensed.